Dear Iz-

This is my most favorite book in the whole world!

Have Mommy read the one on pg 85 "Over The Water" to you — it's about "My Charley."

Anyway, Happy Birthday, very late.

I love you,

George

THE REAL
MOTHER GOOSE

SEE-SAW

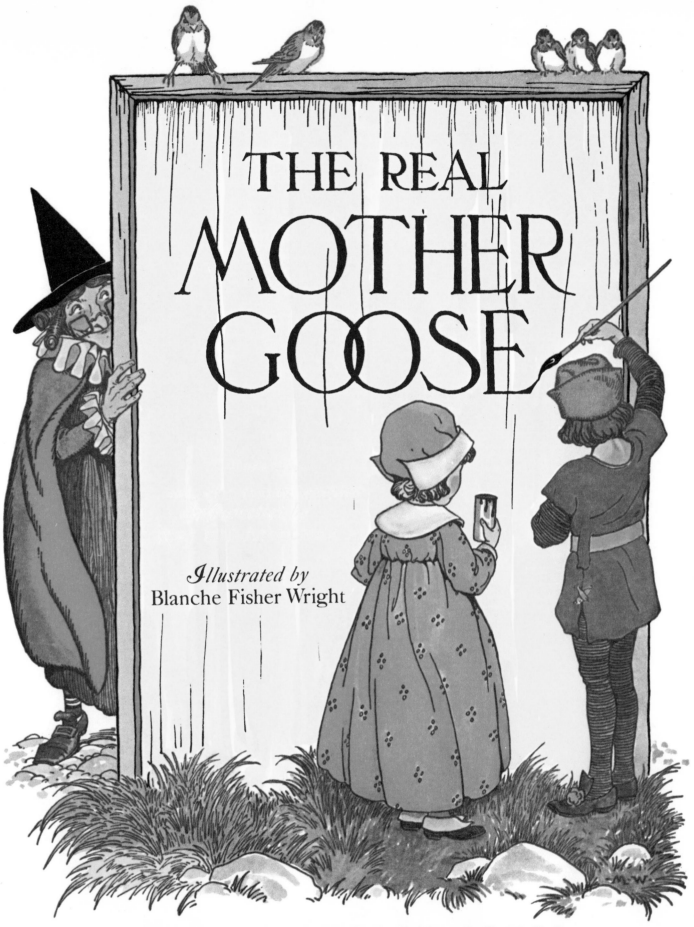

THE REAL
MOTHER
GOOSE

Illustrated by
Blanche Fisher Wright

CHECKERBOARD PRESS
NEW YORK

Mother Goose.
Copyright © 1916, 1944 Checkerboard Press, Inc.
All rights reserved. Printed in U.S.A.
ISBN: 1-56288-041-1

THE REAL MOTHER GOOSE and the black-and-white
checkerboard border design are trademarks of Checkerboard Press, Inc.

Eighty-eighth printing, April 1991
Quality printing and binding by:
Rand McNally
U.S. Bypass 60
Versailles, Kentucky 40383
USA

The Real Mother Goose
1916-1991

As May Hill Arbuthnot observed twenty-five years ago, and it is even more true now, there continues to be an ever-increasing number of books of Mother Goose and nursery rhymes published every year—some on a theme, some demonstrating a noted illustrator's art, some amusing, some scholarly. In these circumstances the continued popularity of THE REAL MOTHER GOOSE after seventy-five years is remarkable. Some of its virtues are obvious. One, of course, is the distinctive black-and-white checkerboard cover, rendering it instantly recognizable to earlier generations, who are eager to share it with young readers. There is the old-fashioned abundance of not only nursery rhymes, but riddles, songs, puzzles, games, fingerplays, sayings and proverbs, tongue twisters, limericks, and counting-out rhymes. The large, clear print, the uncluttered pages, and the traditional but lively illustrations have a timeless charm. But it doesn't really matter how we analyze the popularity of THE REAL MOTHER GOOSE; what is really important is that it continues to find a home with children—to be loved, pored over, endlessly enjoyed.

ANN A. FLOWERS

Editor of The Horn Book Guide to Children's and Young Adult Books

May 12, 1991

May Hill Arbuthnot's 1966 Introduction

IT IS A RARE YEAR in the publishing business that does not yield a new edition of Mother Goose verses, but here is one edition that has survived with fifty years of popularity to its credit. Now Blanche Fisher Wright's THE REAL MOTHER GOOSE is reissued in a special anniversary number for the delight of young children of this and forthcoming generations. That this particular collection of Mother Goose verses has endured is the more surprising considering the amazing variety of editions confronting a prospective buyer. Mother Goose appears with pictures in wild primary colors or pale pastels or blacks and whites. They may be realistic in style or modernistic or old fashioned, or even reproductions of ancient woodcuts. Mother Goose comes fat or thin, tall or small, with a large collection of verses or only a meager few. Why then, with such a variety of books to choose from, should this particular edition have persisted for fifty years? And why, for that matter, has an anonymous collection of ancient rhymes, familiarly known as Mother Goose, continued to delight generations of small fry from the eighteenth century to the present day? First, let's look at the history of the book.

Origins of Mother Goose

Although the verses are as British as plum pudding, the name, Mother Goose, actually made its way into England from France. Perrault's collection of eight famous folk tales in 1697 was called "Contes de ma mère l'Oye" or "Tales of Mother Goose," in short, tall tales or tales of make-believe. These stories were translated into English in 1729. But long after that, when John Newbery and his firm had discovered that such publications for children as their *Little Pretty Pocket-Book* were profitable, they decided to publish a collection of traditional verses and jingles. They gave it the appropriate nonsense name of *Mother Goose's Melody*. This 1791 Newbery edition is one of the rarest of rare books. It contained fifty-two verses, each with an amusing but irrelevant moral added, and each illustrated with a tiny woodcut. This small book concluded with the astonishing addition of sixteen songs from Shakespeare.

In the United States there were pirated editions of the Newbery Mother Goose, one with the picture of a sharp-nosed old crone addressing two children at her knees. After this Mother Goose has denounced all the critics of her ditties she concludes:

> *Fudge! I tell you that all their batterings can't deface my beauties, nor their wise pratings my wiser prattlings; and all imitators of my refreshing songs might as well try to write a new Billy Shakespeare as another Mother Goose—we two great poets were born together, and we shall go out of the world together.*
> *No, no, my Melodies will never die,*
> *While nurses sing, or babies cry.*

A happy and truthful prophecy! An interesting outcome of the Newbery choice of "Mother Goose" as a title for these verses is that it was gradually lost to the famous folk tales which included such immortals as "Cinderella," "Sleeping Beauty" and other favorites, to become more or less permanently attached to this anonymous collection of nursery jingles, identified forevermore as Mother Goose.

Historical Significance of the Verses

There have been books and innumerable articles attaching historical significance to these verses. For example, they say that the "lady upon a white horse" was no less than the first Queen Elizabeth, and Miss Muffet was Mary Queen of Scots frightened by the spider, John Knox. Well, maybe so, but recent research gives small credence to these nebulous guesses. Occasionally, the name of a real person does appear, as Robin Hood or Jack Horner, but history is to be found chiefly in such English place names as Exeter, Gloucester, London Bridge, or in the street cries, old customs, songs, lullabies, games, and the like. These reflect the times and places in which these old jingles developed. Their language also reflects their ancient origin. Children accept "doth" and "thee" and "thou" without a question, but the candle riddle "Little Nancy Etticoat" may need explanation and so will those "Bell horses, bell horses, what time of day?" That is mere sound until the child sees a picture or learns about the huge town clocks where iron horses come prancing out on the stroke of the hour. Barring a few such hurdles, children accept the language and situations of these ancient ditties with placid enjoyment and few questions. Why?

The Ageless Charm of the Verses

The compelling music of these jingles is so ear-catching, children from eighteen months to six years and more will listen to them entranced when they are read aloud. Then, they begin to say them with the reader, and next, they are chanting them when they are alone, never missing a beat or a rhyme. The melodies of these verses may begin crudely with a tumpity-tump sort of beat, but there are also some charming lyrics in Mother Goose collections such as "Daffy-down-dilly," "I saw a ship a-sailing," and others.

The melody and movement of the verses also enhance the action. Everything and everyone seems to be in motion. Jack jumps over the candlestick, the dish runs away with the spoon, a cat comes fiddling out of the barn, and there is a fearless old woman tossed up in a basket "seventeen times high as the moon." No wonder children like these verses. Here is life on the move.

Next to their ear-catching tunes, skipping, hopping, galloping rhythms, and lively action these verses have an inexhaustible variety. There is a crowded gallery of people everyone will remember for the rest of his life—Old King Cole, Jack and Jill, Tommy Tucker, the Queen of Hearts, Jack Horner, and all the rest. The story poems, games, verses about animals make an immediate appeal, and children of five and six enjoy the alphabet and the counting rhymes. Few books offer such diverse entertainment.

Also it is the sheer high spirits of these old jingles, their fun and nonsense that lift the spirits. Children laugh at the cow jumping over the moon, at Peter's wife sitting cozily in a pumpkin shell, at the funny sounds of higgledy, piggledy, sing a song of sixpence, or Peter's peck of pickled peppers. In short they laugh at absurd situations, the grotesque, the funny sounds and the bouncy rhymes and rhythms of the verses.

Finally, it is certainly the illustrations which have always accompanied these old verses that help to spellbind each new generation of children. This brings us to this happy celebration of the fiftieth anniversary of a favorite American edition, illustrated by Blanche Fisher Wright.

The Real Mother Goose

This is a large book, not too large, just good lap size, which means baby and book held comfortably on the lap. Large, clear type and large, clear pictures make it an admirable edition for classroom use. All the illustrations are in color and there are thirty-one full-page pictures, with no distracting details. The sheer drama of "The old woman tossed up in a basket," or the astonished King when "four and twenty blackbirds" come chirping out of his pie, these and many others are going to be remembered. On pages where there are several verses, there may also be as many as three or four bright pictures. There is some humor in these illustrations, but for the most part, they are sober interpretations of the verses. This is a boon to the young child, because the pictures actually furnish him with clues to the meanings of the words. Incidentally, this is a large collection with over three hundred verses. These are some of the reasons why, for the youngest children, THE REAL MOTHER GOOSE is a fine introduction to this collection of wise and witty traditional verses.

So take this handsome book home or to school with you and have fun with it. Read and reread these ditties to your children. Encourage them to speak them with you or alone, savoring their rhymes and rhythms to the full. As a result, children will know more words and speak them more crisply and clearly than they would have without Mother Goose. Above all, they will carry with them some feeling for the fun, freshness and sheer delight of poetry. All this because of Mother Goose.

MAY HILL ARBUTHNOT

WESTERN RESERVE UNIVERSITY

CLEVELAND, OHIO

Author of *Children and Books;*
Time for Poetry; The Arbuthnot Anthology

May 12, 1965

A LIST OF THE RHYMES

(For an alphabetical list of first lines see pp. 7-9)

5

AN ALPHABETICAL LIST OF FIRST LINES

RAIN

THE REAL
MOTHER GOOSE

LITTLE BO-PEEP

Little Bo-Peep has lost her sheep,
    And can't tell where to find
      them;
Leave them alone, and they'll come
    home,
    And bring their tails behind
      them.

Little Bo-Peep fell fast asleep,
    And dreamt she heard them
      bleating;
But when she awoke, she found it
    a joke,
    For still they all were fleeting.

Then up she took her little crook,
    Determined for to find them;
She found them indeed, but it made
    her heart bleed,
    For they'd left all their tails
      behind 'em!

It happened one day, as Bo-peep
    did stray
    Unto a meadow hard by—

There she espied their tails, side
    by side,
    All hung on a tree to dry.

She heaved a sigh and wiped her eye,
    And over the hillocks she
      raced;
And tried what she could, as a
    shepherdess should,
    That each tail should be prop-
      erly placed.

LITTLE BOY BLUE

Little Boy Blue, come, blow your
    horn!
The sheep's in the meadow, the
    cow's in the corn.
Where's the little boy that looks
    after the sheep?
Under the haystack, fast asleep!

RAIN

Rain, rain, go away,
Come again another day;
Little Johnny wants to play.

FINGERS AND TOES

Every lady in this land
Has twenty nails, upon each
    hand
Five, and twenty on hands and
    feet:
All this is true, without deceit.

A SEASONABLE SONG

Piping hot, smoking hot.
    What I've got
    You have not.
Hot gray pease, hot, hot, hot;
Hot gray pease, hot.

THE CLOCK

There's a neat little clock,—
    In the schoolroom it stands,—
And it points to the time
    With its two little hands.

And may we, like the clock,
    Keep a face clean and bright,
With hands ever ready
    To do what is right.

WINTER

Cold and raw the north wind
    doth blow,
Bleak in the morning early;
All the hills are covered with
    snow,
And winter's now come fairly.

DAME TROT AND HER CAT

Dame Trot and her cat
Led a peaceable life,
When they were not troubled
With other folks' strife.

When Dame had her dinner
Pussy would wait,
And was sure to receive
A nice piece from her plate.

THREE CHILDREN ON THE ICE

Three children sliding on the ice
Upon a summer's day,
As it fell out, they all fell in,
The rest they ran away.

Oh, had these children been at
school,
Or sliding on dry ground,
Ten thousand pounds to one penny
They had not then been drowned.

Ye parents who have children dear,
And ye, too, who have none,
If you would keep them safe abroad
Pray keep them safe at home.

CROSS PATCH

Cross patch, draw the latch,
Sit by the fire and spin;
Take a cup and drink it up,
Then call your neighbors in.

THE OLD WOMAN UNDER A HILL

There was an old woman
Lived under a hill;
And if she's not gone,
She lives there still.

TWEEDLE-DUM AND TWEEDLE-DEE

Tweedle-dum and Tweedle-dee
Resolved to have a battle,
For Tweedle-dum said Tweedle-dee
Had spoiled his nice new rattle.

Just then flew by a monstrous crow,
As big as a tar barrel,
Which frightened both the heroes so,
They quite forgot their quarrel.

OH, DEAR!

Dear, dear! what can the matter be?
Two old women got up in an apple-
tree;
One came down, and the other
stayed till Saturday.

OLD MOTHER GOOSE

Old Mother Goose, when
She wanted to wander,
Would ride through the air
On a very fine gander.

LITTLE JUMPING JOAN

Here am I, little jumping Joan,
When nobody's with me
I'm always alone.

PAT-A-CAKE

Pat-a-cake, pat-a-cake,
Baker's man!
So I do, master,
As fast as I can.

Pat it, and prick it,
And mark it with T,
Put it in the oven
For Tommy and me.

MONEY AND THE MARE

"Lend me thy mare to ride a mile."
"She is lamed, leaping over a stile."

"Alack! and I must keep the fair!
I'll give thee money for thy mare."

"Oh, oh! say you so?
Money will make the mare to go!"

ROBIN REDBREAST

Little Robin Redbreast sat upon a tree,
Up went Pussy-Cat, down went he,
Down came Pussy-Cat, away Robin
ran,
Says little Robin Redbreast: "Catch
me if you can!"

Little Robin Redbreast jumped upon
a spade,
Pussy-Cat jumped after him, and
then he was afraid.
Little Robin chirped and sang, and
what did Pussy say?
Pussy-Cat said: "Mew, mew, mew,"
and Robin flew away.

PAT-A-CAKE

A MELANCHOLY SONG

Trip upon trenchers,
And dance upon dishes,
My mother sent me for some barm,
   some barm;
She bid me go lightly,
And come again quickly,
For fear the young men should do
   me some harm.
Yet did n't you see, yet did n't you
   see,
What naughty tricks they put upon
   me?

They broke my
   pitcher
And spilt the
   water,
And huffed my
   mother,
And chid her
   daughter,
And kissed my
   sister instead
   of me.

JACK

Jack be nimble, Jack be
   quick,
Jack jump over the candlestick.

GOING TO ST. IVES

As I was going to St. Ives
I met a man with seven wives.
Every wife had seven sacks,
Every sack had seven cats,
Every cat had seven kits.
Kits, cats, sacks, and wives,
How many were going to St. Ives?

16

BEES

A swarm of bees in May
Is worth a load of hay;
A swarm of bees in June
Is worth a silver spoon;
A swarm of bees in July
Is not worth a fly.

COME OUT TO PLAY

Girls and boys, come out to play,
The moon doth shine as bright as
  day;
Leave your supper, and leave your
  sleep,
And come with your playfellows
  into the street.
Come with a whoop, come with a
  call,
Come with a good will or not at all.
Up the ladder and down the wall,
A half-penny roll will serve us all.
You find milk, and I'll find flour,
And we'll have a pudding in half
  an hour.

THIRTY DAYS HATH SEPTEMBER

Thirty days hath September,
April, June, and November;
February has twenty-eight alone,
All the rest have thirty-one,
Excepting leap-year, that's the time
When February's days are twenty-
  nine.

BABY DOLLY

Hush, baby, my dolly, I pray you
  don't cry,
And I'll give you some bread, and
  some milk by-and-by;
Or perhaps you like custard, or,
  maybe, a tart,
Then to either you're welcome, with
  all my heart.

TO MARKET, TO MARKET, TO BUY A FAT PIG

IF WISHES WERE HORSES

If wishes were horses, beggars would
    ride.
If turnips were watches, I would
    wear one by my side.
    And if "ifs" and "ands"
    Were pots and pans,
There'd be no work for tinkers!

TO MARKET

To market, to market, to buy a fat
    pig,
Home again, home again, jiggety jig.
To market, to market, to buy a fat
    hog,
Home again, home again, jiggety
    jog.
To market, to market, to buy a plum
    bun,
Home again, home again, market is
    done.

OLD CHAIRS TO MEND

If I'd as much money as I could
    spend,
I never would cry old chairs to
    mend;
Old chairs to mend, old chairs to
    mend;
I never would cry old chairs to mend.

If I'd as much money as I could
    tell,
I never would cry old clothes to
    sell;
Old clothes to sell, old clothes to
    sell;
I never would cry old clothes to sell.

ROBIN AND RICHARD

Robin and Richard were two pretty men,
They lay in bed till the clock struck ten;
Then up starts Robin and looks at the sky,
"Oh, brother Richard, the sun's very high!
You go before, with the bottle and bag,
And I will come after on little Jack Nag."

A MAN AND A MAID

There was a little man,
Who wooed a little maid,
And he said, "Little maid, will you
 wed, wed, wed?
I have little more to say,
So will you, yea or nay,
For least said is soonest mended-ded,
 ded, ded."

The little maid replied,
 "Should I be your little bride,
Pray what must we have for to eat,
 eat, eat?
Will the flame that you're so
 rich in
Light a fire in the kitchen?
Or the little god of love turn the
 spit, spit, spit?"

HERE GOES MY LORD

Here goes my lord
A trot, a trot, a trot, a trot,
 Here goes my lady
A canter, a canter, a canter, a canter!

 Here goes my young master
Jockey-hitch, jockey-hitch, jockey-
 hitch, jockey-hitch!
 Here goes my young miss
An amble, an amble, an amble, an
 amble!

The footman lags behind to tipple
 ale and wine,
And goes gallop, a gallop, a gallop,
 to make up his time.

THE CLEVER HEN

I had a little hen, the prettiest
 ever seen,
She washed me the dishes and
 kept the house clean;
She went to the mill to fetch me
 some flour,
She brought it home in less than
 an hour;
She baked me my bread, she
 brewed me my ale,
She sat by the fire and told
 many a fine tale.

LUCY LOCKET

TWO BIRDS

There were two birds sat on a stone,
    Fa, la, la, la, lal, de;
One flew away, and then there was
    one,
    Fa, la, la, la, lal, de;
The other bird flew after,
And then there was none,
    Fa, la, la, la, lal, de;
And so the stone
Was left alone,
    Fa, la, la, la, lal, de.

LEG OVER LEG

Leg over leg,
As the dog went to Dover;
When he came to a stile,
Jump, he went over.

LUCY LOCKET

Lucy Locket lost her pocket,
Kitty Fisher found it;
Nothing in it, nothing in it,
But the binding round it.

WHEN JENNY WREN WAS YOUNG

'Twas once upon a time, when
    Jenny Wren was young,
So daintily she danced and so pret-
    tily she sung,
Robin Redbreast lost his heart, for
    he was a gallant bird.
So he doffed his hat to Jenny Wren,
    requesting to be heard.

"Oh, dearest Jenny Wren, if you
    will but be mine,
You shall feed on cherry pie and
    drink new currant wine,
I'll dress you like a goldfinch or any
    peacock gay,
So, dearest Jen, if you'll be mine, let
    us appoint the day."

Jenny blushed behind her fan and
    thus declared her mind:
"Since, dearest Bob, I love you well,
    I'll take your offer kind.
Cherry pie is very nice and so is
    currant wine,
But I must wear my plain brown
    gown and never go too fine."

SOLOMON GRUNDY

Solomon Grundy,
Born on a Monday,
Christened on Tuesday,
Married on Wednesday,
Took ill on Thursday,
Worse on Friday,
Died on Saturday,
Buried on Sunday.
This is the end
Of Solomon Grundy.

BARBER

Barber, barber, shave a pig.
How many hairs will make a wig?
Four and twenty; that's enough.
Give the barber a pinch of snuff.

THE FLYING PIG

Dickory, dickory, dare,
The pig flew up in the air;
The man in brown soon brought
    him down,
      Dickory,
        dickory,
          dare.

HUSH-A-BYE

Hush-a-bye, baby, on the tree top!
When the wind blows the cradle
    will rock;
When the bough breaks the cradle
    will fall;
Down will come baby, bough, cradle
    and all.

BURNIE BEE

Burnie bee, burnie bee,
Tell me when your wedding be?
If it be to-morrow day,
Take your wings and fly away.

THREE WISE MEN OF GOTHAM

Three wise men of Gotham
Went to sea in a bowl;
If the bowl had been stronger
My song had been longer.

THE HUNTER OF REIGATE

A man went a-hunting at Reigate,
And wished to leap over a high
    gate.
Says the owner, "Go round,
With your gun and your hound,
For you never shall leap over my
    gate."

PIPPEN HILL

As I was going up Pippen Hill,
    Pippen Hill was dirty;
There I met a pretty Miss,
    And she dropped me a
        curtsy.

Little Miss, pretty Miss,
    Blessings light upon you;
If I had half-a-crown a day,
    I'd spend it all upon you.

LITTLE POLLY FLINDERS

Little Polly Flinders
Sat among the cinders
    Warming her pretty little toes;
Her mother came and caught her,
Whipped her little daughter
    For spoiling her nice new
        clothes.

RIDE AWAY, RIDE AWAY

Ride away, ride away,
    Johnny shall ride,
And he shall have pussy-cat
    Tied to one side;
And he shall have little dog
    Tied to the other,
And Johnny shall ride
    To see his grandmother.

PUSSY-CAT AND QUEEN

"Pussy-cat, pussy-cat,
    Where have you been?"
"I've been to London
    To look at the Queen."

"Pussy-cat, pussy-cat,
    What did you there?"
"I frightened a little mouse
    Under the chair."

THE WINDS

Mister East gave a feast;
Mister North laid the cloth;
Mister West did his best;
Mister South burnt his mouth
Eating cold potato.

26

PUSSY-CAT AND QUEEN

CLAP HANDIES

Clap, clap handies,

Mammie's wee, wee ain;

Clap, clap handies,

Daddie's comin' hame,

Hame till his bonny wee bit laddie;

Clap, clap handies,

My wee, wee ain.

CHRISTMAS

Christmas comes but once a year,

And when it comes it brings good
cheer.

ELIZABETH

Elizabeth, Elspeth, Betsy, and
Bess,

They all went together to seek a
bird's nest;

They found a bird's nest with five
eggs in,

They all took one, and left four in.

JUST LIKE ME

"I went up one pair of stairs."
"Just like me."

"I went up two pairs of stairs."
"Just like me."

"I went into a room."
"Just like me."

"I looked out of a window."
"Just like me."

"And there I saw a monkey."
"Just like me."

PLAY DAYS

How many days has my baby to
play?

Saturday, Sunday, Monday,

Tuesday, Wednesday, Thursday,
Friday,

Saturday, Sunday, Monday.

HEIGH-HO, THE CARRION CROW

A carrion crow sat on an oak,
  Fol de riddle, lol de riddle,
  hi ding do,
Watching a tailor shape his
  cloak;
    Sing heigh-ho, the carrion
    crow,
    Fol de riddle, lol de riddle,
    hi ding do!

Wife, bring me my old bent bow,
  Fol de riddle, lol de riddle,
  hi ding do,
That I may shoot yon carrion
  crow;
    Sing heigh-ho, the carrion
    crow,
    Fol de riddle, lol de riddle,
    hi ding do!

The tailor he shot, and missed
  his mark,
  Fol de riddle, lol de riddle,
  hi ding do!
And shot his own sow quite
  through the heart;
    Sing heigh-ho, the carrion crow,
    Fol de riddle, lol de riddle,
    hi ding do!

Wife! bring brandy in a spoon,
  Fol de riddle, lol de riddle,
  hi ding do!
For our old sow is in a swoon;
    Sing heigh-ho, the carrion
    crow,
    Fol de riddle, lol de riddle,
    hi ding do!

29

BANBURY CROSS

Ride a cock-horse to Banbury Cross,
To see an old lady upon a white
    horse.
Rings on her fingers, and bells on
    her toes,
She shall have music wherever she
    goes.

THE MAN IN OUR TOWN

There was a man in our town,
    And he was wondrous wise,
He jumped into a bramble bush,
    And scratched out both his
        eyes;
But when he saw his eyes were out,
    With all his might and main,
He jumped into another bush,
    And scratched 'em in again.

A B C

Great A, little a,
    Bouncing B!
The cat's in the cupboard,
    And can't see me.

A NEEDLE AND THREAD

Old Mother Twitchett had but
    one eye,
And a long tail which she let fly;
And every time she went through
    a gap,
A bit of her tail she left in a trap.

RIDE A COCK-HORSE TO BANBURY CROSS

GEORGY PORGY

Georgy Porgy, pudding and pie,
Kissed the girls and made them cry.
When the boys came out to play,
Georgy Porgy ran away.

FOR EVERY EVIL

For every evil under the sun
There is a remedy or there is none.
If there be one, seek till you find it;
If there be none, never mind it.

CUSHY COW

Cushy cow, bonny, let down thy milk,
And I will give thee a gown of silk;
A gown of silk and a silver tee,
If thou wilt let down thy milk to me.

WEE WILLIE WINKIE

Wee Willie Winkie runs through
    the town,
Upstairs and downstairs, in his
    nightgown;
Rapping at the window, crying
    through the lock,
"Are the children in their beds?
    Now it's eight o'clock."

ABOUT THE BUSH

About the bush, Willie,
    About the beehive,
About the bush, Willie,
    I'll meet thee alive.

SEE-SAW

See-saw, Margery Daw,
Sold her bed and lay upon straw.

ROBIN-A-BOBBIN

Robin-a-Bobbin
Bent his bow,
Shot at a pigeon,
And killed a crow.

JOHN SMITH

Is John Smith within?
Yes, that he is.
Can he set a shoe?
Ay, marry, two.
Here a nail, there a nail,
Tick, tack, too.

THREE BLIND MICE

SIMPLE SIMON

Simple Simon met a pieman,
    Going to the fair;
Says Simple Simon to the pieman,
    "Let me taste your ware."

Says the pieman to Simple Simon,
    "Show me first your penny,"
Says Simple Simon to the pieman,
    "Indeed, I have not any."

Simple Simon went a-fishing
    For to catch a whale;
All the water he could find
    Was in his mother's pail!

Simple Simon went to look
    If plums grew on a thistle;
He pricked his fingers very much,
    Which made poor Simon
        whistle.

He went to catch a dicky bird,
    And thought he could not fail,
Because he had a little salt,
    To put upon its tail.

He went for water with a sieve,
    But soon it ran all through;
And now poor Simple Simon
    Bids you all adieu.

THREE BLIND MICE

Three blind mice! See how they run!
They all ran after the farmer's wife,
Who cut off their tails with a carv-
    ing knife.
Did you ever see such a thing in
    your life
As three blind mice?

FIVE TOES

This little pig went to market;
This little pig stayed at home;
This little pig had roast beef;
This little pig had none;
This little pig said, "Wee, wee!
I can't find my way home."

The drake was a-swimming with
his curly tail;
The little man made it his mark,
mark, mark.
He let off his gun, but he fired
too soon,
And the drake flew away with a
quack, quack, quack.

DOCTOR FOSTER

Doctor Foster went to Glo'ster,
In a shower of rain;
He stepped in a puddle, up to his
middle,
And never went there again.

A LITTLE MAN

There was a little man, and he had
a little gun,
And his bullets were made of
lead, lead, lead;
He went to the brook, and saw a
little duck,
And shot it right through the
head, head, head.

He carried it home to his old wife
Joan,
And bade her a fire to make,
make, make.
To roast the little duck he had shot
in the brook,
And he'd go and fetch the drake,
drake, drake.

DIDDLE DIDDLE DUMPLING

Diddle diddle dumpling, my son John
Went to bed with his breeches on,
One stocking off, and one stocking on;
Diddle diddle dumpling, my son John.

JERRY HALL

Jerry Hall, he was so small,
A rat could eat him, hat and all.

LENGTHENING DAYS

As the days grow longer
The storms grow stronger.

CURLY-LOCKS, CURLY-LOCKS, WILT THOU BE MINE?

THE BLACK HEN

Hickety, pickety, my black hen,
She lays eggs for gentlemen;
Gentlemen come every day
To see what my black hen
    doth lay.

THE MIST

A hill full, a hole full,
Yet you cannot catch a bowl full.

A CANDLE

Little Nanny Etticoat
In a white petticoat,
And a red nose;
The longer she stands
The shorter she grows.

MISS MUFFET

Little Miss Muffet
Sat on a tuffet,
Eating of curds and whey;
    There came a big spider,
    And sat down beside her,
And frightened Miss Muffet away.

CURLY-LOCKS

Curly-locks, Curly-locks, wilt thou be mine?
Thou shalt not wash the dishes, nor yet feed
    the swine;
But sit on a cushion, and sew a fine seam,
And feed upon strawberries, sugar, and
    cream.

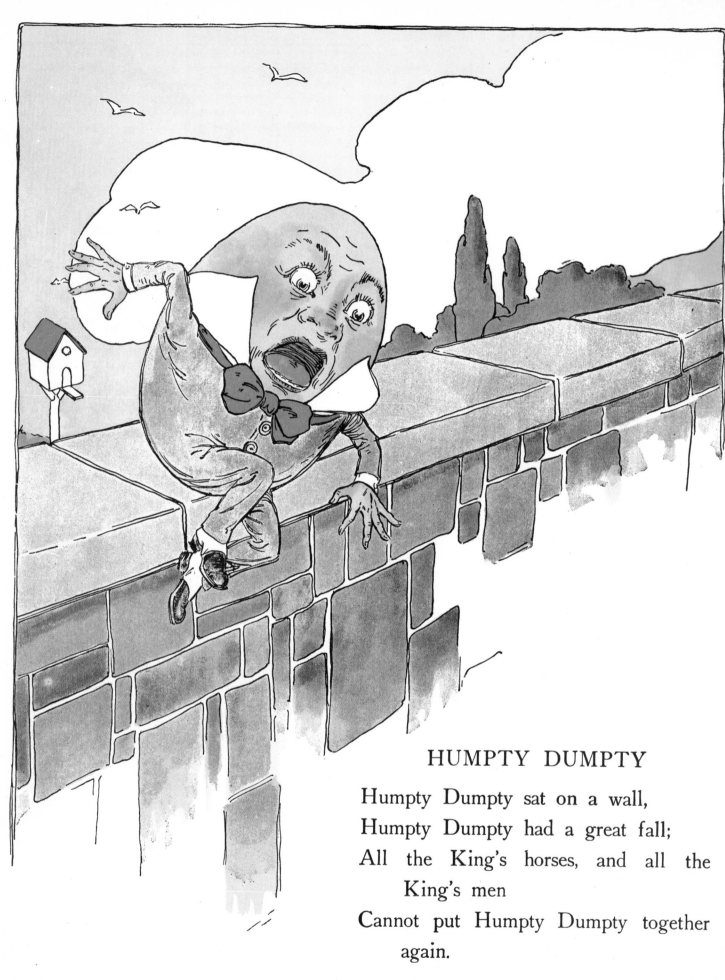

HUMPTY DUMPTY

Humpty Dumpty sat on a wall,
Humpty Dumpty had a great fall;
All the King's horses, and all the
    King's men
Cannot put Humpty Dumpty together
    again.

40

ONE, TWO, THREE

One, two, three, four, five,
Once I caught a fish alive.
Six, seven, eight, nine, ten,
But I let it go again.
Why did you let it go?
Because it bit my finger so.
Which finger did it bite?
The little one upon the right.

THE DOVE AND THE WREN

The dove says coo, coo, what shall
    I do?
I can scarce maintain two.
Pooh, pooh! says the wren, I've got
    ten,
And keep them all like gentlemen.

MASTER I HAVE

Master I have, and I am his man,
    Gallop a dreary dun;
Master I have, and I am his man,
    And I'll get a wife as fast as
    I can;
With a heighty gaily gamberally,
    Higgledy piggledy, niggledy,
    niggledy,
    Gallop a dreary dun.

PINS

See a pin and pick it up,
All the day you'll have good luck.
See a pin and let it lay,
Bad luck you'll have all the day.

SHALL WE GO A-SHEARING?

"Old woman, old woman, shall we
    go a-shearing?"
"Speak a little louder, sir, I am
    very thick of hearing."
"Old woman, old woman, shall I
    kiss you dearly?"
"Thank you, kind sir, I hear you
    very clearly."

GOOSEY, GOOSEY, GANDER

GOOSEY, GOOSEY, GANDER

Goosey, goosey, gander,
 Whither dost thou wander?
Upstairs and downstairs
 And in my lady's chamber.

There I met an old man
 Who would n't say his prayers;
I took him by the left leg,
 And threw him down the stairs.

OLD MOTHER HUBBARD

Old Mother Hubbard
Went to the cupboard,
 To give her poor dog a bone;
But when she got there
The cupboard was bare,
 And so the poor dog had none.

She went to the baker's
 To buy him some bread;
When she came back
 The dog was dead.

She went to the undertaker's
 To buy him a coffin;
When she got back
 The dog was laughing.

She took a clean dish
 To get him some tripe;
When she came back
 He was smoking a pipe.

She went to the alehouse
 To get him some beer;
When she came back
 The dog sat in a chair.

She went to the tavern
 For white wine and red;
When she came back
 The dog stood on his head.

She went to the hatter's
 To buy him a hat;
When she came back
 He was feeding the cat.

She went to the barber's
 To buy him a wig;
When she came back
 He was dancing a jig.

She went to the fruiterer's
 To buy him some fruit;
When she came back
 He was playing the flute.

She went to the tailor's
 To buy him a coat;
When she came back
 He was riding a goat.

She went to the cobbler's
 To buy him some shoes;
When she came back
 He was reading the news.

She went to the sempster's
   To buy him some linen;
When she came back
   The dog was a-spinning.

She went to the hosier's
   To buy him some hose;
When she came back
   He was dressed in his clothes.

The dame made a curtsy,
   The dog made a bow;
The dame said, "Your servant,"
   The dog said, "Bow-wow."

THE COCK AND THE HEN

"Cock, cock, cock, cock,
   I've laid an egg,
   Am I to gang ba—are-foot?"

"Hen, hen, hen, hen,
   I've been up and down
   To every shop in town,
   And cannot find a shoe
   To fit your foot,
   If I'd crow my hea—art out."

BLUE BELL BOY

I had a little boy,
   And called him Blue Bell;
Gave him a little work,—
   He did it very well.

I bade him go upstairs
   To bring me a gold pin;
In coal scuttle fell he,
   Up to his little chin.

He went to the garden
   To pick a little sage;
He tumbled on his nose,
   And fell into a rage.

He went to the cellar
   To draw a little beer;
And quickly did return
   To say there was none there.

WHY MAY NOT I LOVE JOHNNY?

Johnny shall have a new bonnet,
  And Johnny shall go to the fair,
And Johnny shall have a blue ribbon
  To tie up his bonny brown hair.

And why may not I love Johnny?
  And why may not Johnny
    love me?
And why may not I love Johnny
  As well as another body?

And here's a leg for a stocking,
  And here's a foot for a shoe,
And he has a kiss for his daddy,
  And two for his mammy, I trow.

And why may not I love Johnny?
  And why may not Johnny love
    me?
And why may not I love Johnny
  As well as another body?

JACK JELF

Little Jack Jelf
Was put on the shelf
Because he could not spell "pie";
  When his aunt, Mrs. Grace,
  Saw his sorrowful face,
She could not help saying, "Oh, fie!"

And since Master Jelf
Was put on the shelf
Because he could not spell "pie,"
  Let him stand there so grim,
  And no more about him,
For I wish him a very good-bye!

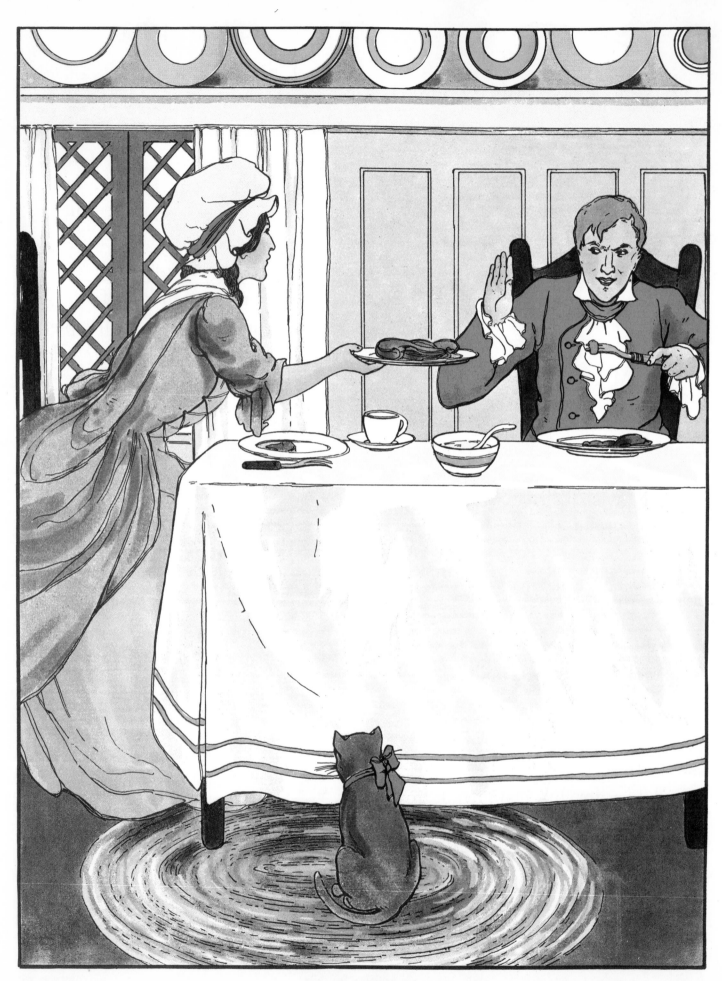

JACK SPRAT

JACK SPRAT

Jack Sprat
　　Could eat no fat,
His wife could eat no lean;
　　And so,
　　Betwixt them both,
They licked the platter clean.

HUSH-A-BYE

Hush-a-bye, baby,
　　Daddy is near;
Mamma is a lady,
　　And that's very clear.

DAFFODILS

Daffy-down-dilly has come to town
In a yellow petticoat and a green
　　gown.

THE GIRL IN THE LANE

The girl in the lane, that couldn't
　　speak plain,
　　Cried, "Gobble, gobble, gobble":
The man on the hill that couldn't
　　stand still,
　　Went hobble hobble, hobble.

HUSH-A-BYE

Hush-a-bye, baby, lie still with thy
　　daddy,
　　Thy mammy has gone to the
　　mill,
To get some meal to bake a cake,
　　So pray, my dear baby, lie still.

NANCY DAWSON

Nancy Dawson was so fine
She wouldn't get up to serve the swine;
She lies in bed till eight or nine,
So it's Oh, poor Nancy Dawson.

And do ye ken Nancy Dawson, honey?
The wife who sells the barley, honey?
She won't get up to feed her swine,
And do ye ken Nancy Dawson, honey?

HANDY PANDY

Handy Pandy, Jack-a-dandy,
Loves plum cake and sugar candy.
He bought some at a grocer's shop,
And out he came, hop, hop, hop!

JACK AND JILL

Jack and Jill went up the hill,
    To fetch a pail of water;
Jack fell down, and broke his crown,
    And Jill came tumbling after.

Then up Jack got and off did trot,
    As fast as he could caper,
To old Dame Dob, who patched his
        nob
    With vinegar and brown paper.

THE ALPHABET

A, B, C, and D,
Pray, playmates, agree.
E, F, and G,
Well, so it shall be.
J, K, and L,
In peace we will dwell.
M, N, and O,
To play let us go.
P, Q, R, and S,
Love may we possess.
W, X, and Y,
Will not quarrel or die.
Z, and ampersand,
Go to school at command.

DANCE TO YOUR DADDIE

Dance to your daddie,
My bonnie laddie;
Dance to your daddie, my bonnie
    lamb;
You shall get a fishy,
On a little dishy;
You shall get a fishy, when the boat
    comes home.

ONE MISTY MOISTY MORNING

One misty moisty morning,
    When cloudy was the weather,
I chanced to meet an old man,
    Clothed all in leather.
He began to compliment
    And I began to grin.
How do you do? And how do you do?
    And how do you do again?

ROBIN HOOD AND LITTLE JOHN

Robin Hood, Robin Hood,
    Is in the mickle wood!
Little John, Little John,
    He to the town is gone.

Robin Hood, Robin Hood,
    Telling his beads,
All in the greenwood
    Among the green weeds.
Little John, Little John,
    If he comes no more,
Robin Hood, Robin Hood,
    We shall fret full sore!

RAIN

Rain, rain, go to Spain,
And never come back again.

ROBIN HOOD

THE ROBINS

A robin and a robin's son
Once went to town to buy a bun.
They couldn't decide on plum or
    plain,
And so they went back home again.

THE OLD MAN

There was an old man
In a velvet coat,
He kissed a maid
And gave her a groat.
The groat it was crack'd
And would not go,—
Ah, old man, do you serve me so?

THE OLD WOMAN FROM FRANCE

There came an old woman from
    France
Who taught grown-up children to
    dance;
    But they were so stiff,
    She sent them home in a sniff,
This sprightly old woman from
    France.

TEETH AND GUMS

Thirty white horses upon a red hill,
Now they tramp, now they champ,
    now they stand still.

IF ALL THE SEAS WERE ONE SEA

If all the seas were one sea,
What a *great* sea that would be!
And if all the trees were one tree,
What a *great* tree that would be!
And if all the axes were one axe,
What a *great* axe that would be!
And if all the men were one man,
What a *great* man he would be!
And if the *great* man took the *great*
        axe,
And cut down the *great* tree,
And let it fall into the *great* sea,
What a splish splash *that* would be!

T'OTHER LITTLE TUNE

I won't be my father's Jack,
    I won't be my father's Jill;
I will be the fiddler's wife,
    And have music when I will.
        T'other little tune,
        T'other little tune,
        Prithee, Love, play me
        T'other little tune.

MY KITTEN

Hey, my kitten, my kitten,
    And hey, my kitten, my deary!
Such a sweet pet as this
    Was neither far nor neary.

HERE SITS THE LORD MAYOR

HERE SITS THE LORD MAYOR

FOREHEAD, EYES, CHEEKS, NOSE, MOUTH, AND CHIN

Here sits the Lord Mayor,
　　Here sit his two men,
Here sits the cock,
　　Here sits the hen,
Here sit the little chickens,
　　Here they run in.
Chin-chopper, chin-chopper, chin
　　chopper, chin!

TWO PIGEONS

I had two pigeons bright and gay,
They flew from me the other day.
What was the reason they did go?
I cannot tell, for I do not know.

PANCAKE DAY

Great A, little a,
This is pancake day;
Toss the ball high,
Throw the ball low,
Those that come after
May sing heigh-ho!

A PLUM PUDDING

Flour of England, fruit of Spain,
　　Met together in a shower of rain;
Put in a bag tied round with a
　　string;
If you'll tell me this riddle,
　　I'll give you a ring.

A SURE TEST

If you are to be a gentleman,
As I suppose you'll be,
You'll neither laugh nor smile,
For a tickling of the knee.

LOCK AND KEY

"I am a gold lock."
"I am a gold key."
"I am a silver lock."
"I am a silver key."
"I am a brass lock."
"I am a brass key."
"I am a lead lock."
"I am a lead key."
"I am a don lock."
"I am a don key!"

THE LION AND THE UNICORN

The Lion and the Unicorn were
fighting for the crown,
The Lion beat the Unicorn all
around the town.
Some gave them white bread, and
some gave them brown,
Some gave them plum-cake, and
sent them out of town.

THE MERCHANTS OF LONDON

Hey diddle dinkety poppety pet,
The merchants of London they wear
scarlet,
Silk in the collar and gold in the
hem,
So merrily march the merchant
men.

I HAD A LITTLE HUSBAND

I had a little husband no bigger
    than my thumb,
I put him in a pint pot, and there
    I bid him drum,
I bought a little handkerchief to
    wipe his little nose,
And a pair of little garters to tie his
    little hose.

TO BABYLON

How many miles is it to Babylon?—
    Threescore miles and ten.
Can I get there by candle-light?—
    Yes, and back again.
If your heels are nimble and light,
You may get there by candle-light.

I'LL TELL YOU A STORY

I'll tell you a story
About Jack-a-Nory:
And now my story's begun.
I'll tell you another
About his brother:
And now my story is done.

A STRANGE OLD WOMAN

There was an old woman, and what
    do you think?
She lived upon nothing but victuals
    and drink;
Victuals and drink were the chief
    of her diet,
And yet this old woman could
    never be quiet.

BAA, BAA, BLACK SHEEP

Baa, baa, black sheep,
Have you any wool?
Yes, marry, have I,
Three bags full;

One for my master,
One for my dame,
But none for the little boy
Who cries in the lane.

LITTLE FRED

When little Fred went to bed,
He always said his prayers;
He kissed mamma, and then papa,
And straightway went upstairs.

SLEEP, BABY, SLEEP

Sleep, baby, sleep,
Our cottage vale is deep:
The little lamb is on the green,
With woolly fleece so soft and clean—
Sleep, baby, sleep.

Sleep, baby, sleep,
Down where the woodbines creep;
Be always like the lamb so mild,
A kind, and sweet, and gentle child.
Sleep, baby, sleep.

CRY, BABY

Cry, baby, cry,
Put your finger in your eye,
And tell your mother it wasn't I.

BAA, BAA, BLACK SHEEP

THE CAT AND THE FIDDLE

Hey, diddle, diddle!
The cat and the fiddle,
The cow jumped over the moon;
The little dog laughed
To see such sport,
And the dish ran away with the spoon.

DOCTOR FELL

I do not like thee, Doctor Fell;
The reason why I cannot tell;
But this I know, and know full well,
I do not like thee, Doctor Fell!

A COUNTING-OUT RHYME

Hickery, dickery, 6 and 7,
Alabone, Crackabone, 10 and 11,
Spin, spun, muskidun,
Twiddle 'em, twaddle 'em, 21.

JACK AND HIS FIDDLE

"Jacky, come and give me thy fiddle,
  If ever thou mean to thrive."
"Nay, I'll not give my fiddle
  To any man alive.

"If I should give my fiddle,
  They'll think that I've gone mad;
For many a joyous day
  My fiddle and I have had."

BUTTONS

Buttons, a farthing a pair!
Come, who will buy them of me?
They're round and sound and pretty,
And fit for girls of the city.
Come, who will buy them of me?
Buttons, a farthing a pair!

HOT BOILED BEANS

Ladies and gentlemen come to
  supper—
Hot boiled beans and very good
  butter.

61

When the pie was opened
   The birds began to sing;
Was not that a dainty dish
   To set before the king?

The king was in his counting-house,
   Counting out his money;
The queen was in the parlor,
   Eating bread and honey.

The maid was in the garden,
   Hanging out the clothes;
When down came a blackbird
   And snapped off her nose.

LITTLE PUSSY

I like little Pussy,
   Her coat is so warm,
And if I don't hurt her
   She'll do me no harm;
So I'll not pull her tail,
   Nor drive her away,
But Pussy and I
   Very gently will play.

SING A SONG OF SIXPENCE

Sing a song of sixpence,
   A pocket full of rye;
Four-and-twenty blackbirds
   Baked in a pie!

SING A SONG OF SIXPENCE

The horns that grew on his head, sir,
  they were so wondrous high,
As I've been plainly told, sir, they
  reached up to the sky.
  The sky, the sky, the sky;
As I've been plainly told, sir, they
  reached up to the sky.

The tail that grew from his back, sir,
  was six yards and an ell;
And it was sent to Derby to toll the
  market bell;
  The bell, the bell, the bell;
And it was sent to Derby to toll
  the market bell.

TOMMY TITTLEMOUSE

Little Tommy Tittlemouse
Lived in a little house;
He caught fishes
In other men's ditches.

THE DERBY RAM

As I was going to Derby all on a
  market-day,
I met the finest ram, sir, that ever
  was fed upon hay;
  Upon hay, upon hay, upon hay;
I met the finest ram, sir, that ever
  was fed upon hay.
This ram was fat behind, sir; this
  ram was fat before;
This ram was ten yards round, sir;
  indeed, he was no more;
  No more, no more, no more;
This ram was ten yards round, sir;
  indeed, he was no more.

This is the way we wash our clothes,
On a cold and frosty morning.

This is the way we go to school,
Go to school, go to school,
This is the way we go to school,
On a cold and frosty morning.

This is the way we come out of school,
Come out of school, come out of
    school,
This is the way we come out of
    school,
On a cold and frosty morning.

THE HOBBY-HORSE

I had a little hobby-horse,
    And it was dapple gray;
Its head was made of pea-straw,
    Its tail was made of hay.

I sold it to an old woman
    For a copper groat;
And I'll not sing my song again
    Without another coat.

THE MULBERRY BUSH

Here we go round the mulberry bush,
The mulberry bush, the mulberry
    bush,
Here we go round the mulberry bush.
On a cold and frosty morning.

This is the way we wash our hands,
Wash our hands, wash our hands,
This is the way we wash our hands,
On a cold and frosty morning.

This is the way we wash our clothes.
Wash our clothes, wash our clothes,

YOUNG LAMBS TO SELL

If I'd as much money as I could tell,
I never would cry young lambs to sell;
Young lambs to sell, young lambs to sell;
I never would cry young lambs to sell.

OLD WOMAN, OLD WOMAN

There was an old woman tossed in
    a basket,
    Seventeen times as high as the
      moon;
But where she was going no mortal
    could tell,
    For under her arm she carried a
      broom.
"Old woman, old woman, old
    woman," said I,
    "Whither, oh whither, oh whither
    so high?"
"To sweep the cobwebs from the sky;
    And I'll be with you by-and-by."

THE FIRST OF MAY

The fair maid who, the first of May,
Goes to the fields at break of day,
And washes in dew from the haw-
    thorn-tree,
Will ever after handsome be.

BOY AND THE SPARROW

A little cock-sparrow sat on a green
    tree,
And he chirruped, he chirruped, so
    merry was he;
A naughty boy came with his wee
    bow and arrow,
Determined to shoot this little cock-
    sparrow.
"This little cock-sparrow shall make
    me a stew,
And his giblets shall make me a
    little pie, too."
"Oh, no," says the sparrow "I won't
    make a stew."
So he flapped his wings and away
    he flew.

THE OLD WOMAN TOSSED IN A BASKET

SULKY SUE

Here's Sulky Sue,
What shall we do?
Turn her face to the wall
Till she comes to.

THE HOUSE THAT JACK BUILT

This is the house that Jack built.
This is the malt
That lay in the house that Jack built.

This is the rat,
That ate the malt
That lay in the house that Jack built.

This is the cat,
That killed the rat,

That ate the malt
That lay in the house that Jack built.

This is the dog,
That worried the cat,
That killed the rat,
That ate the malt
That lay in the house that Jack built.

This is the cow with the crumpled horn,
That tossed the dog,
That worried the cat,
That killed the rat,
That ate the malt
That lay in the house that Jack built.

This is the maiden all forlorn,
That milked the cow with the crumpled horn,
That tossed the dog,
That worried the cat,
That killed the rat,
That ate the malt
That lay in the house that Jack built

This is the man all tattered and torn,
That kissed the maiden all forlorn,
That milked the cow with the crumpled horn,
That tossed the dog,
That worried the cat,
That killed the rat,

That ate the malt

That lay in the house that Jack
built.

This is the priest all shaven and
shorn,

That married the man all tattered
and torn,

That kissed the maiden all forlorn,

That milked the cow with the
crumpled horn,

That tossed the dog,

That worried the cat,

That killed the rat,

That ate the malt

That lay in the house that Jack
built.

This is the cock that crowed in the
morn,

That waked the priest all shaven
and shorn,

That married the man all tattered
and torn,

That kissed the maiden all forlorn,

That milked the cow with the
crumpled horn,

That tossed the dog,

That worried the cat,

That killed the rat,

That ate the malt

That lay in the house that Jack
built.

This is the farmer sowing the corn,

That kept the cock that crowed in
the morn.

That waked the priest all shaven
and shorn,

That married the man all tattered
and torn,

That kissed the maiden all forlorn,

That milked the cow with the
crumpled horn,

That tossed the dog,

That worried the cat,

That killed the rat,

That ate the malt

That lay in the house that Jack built.

SATURDAY, SUNDAY

On Saturday night
    Shall be all my care
To powder my locks
    And curl my hair.

On Sunday morning
    My love will come in,
When he will marry me
    With a gold ring.

69

THE OLD WOMAN AND THE PEDLAR

LITTLE JENNY WREN

Little Jenny Wren fell sick,
    Upon a time;
In came Robin Redbreast
    And brought her cake and
      wine.

"Eat well of my cake, Jenny,
    Drink well of my wine."
"Thank you, Robin, kindly,
    You shall be mine."

Jenny she got well,
    And stood upon her feet,
And told Robin plainly
    She loved him not a bit.

Robin being angry,
    Hopped upon a twig,
Saying, "Out upon you! Fie upon
      you!
    Bold-faced jig!"

THE OLD WOMAN AND THE PEDLAR

There was an old woman, as I've
    heard tell,
She went to market her eggs for to
    sell;
She went to market all on a market-
    day,
And she fell asleep on the King's
    highway.

There came by a pedlar whose
    name was Stout,
He cut her petticoats all round
    about;
He cut her petticoats up to the
    knees,
Which made the old woman to shiver
    and freeze.

When the little old woman first did
    wake,
She began to shiver and she began
    to shake;
She began to wonder and she began
    to cry,
"Lauk a mercy on me, this can't
    be I!

"But if it be I, as I hope it be,
I've a little dog at home, and he'll
    know me;
If it be I, he'll wag his little tail,
And if it be not I, he'll loudly bark
    and wail."

Home went the little woman all in
    the dark;
Up got the little dog, and he began
    to bark;
He began to bark, so she began to
    cry,
"Lauk a mercy on me, this is none
    of I!"

BOBBY SNOOKS

Little Bobby Snooks was fond of
    his books,
    And loved by his usher and mas-
        ter;
But naughty Jack Spry, he got a
    black eye,
    And carries his nose in a plaster.

THE LITTLE MOPPET

I had a little moppet,
I put it in my pocket,
And fed it with corn and hay.
    There came a proud beggar.
    And swore he should have her;
And stole my little moppet away.

I SAW A SHIP A-SAILING

I saw a ship a-sailing,
A-sailing on the sea;
And, oh! it was all laden
With pretty things for thee!

There were comfits in the cabin,
And apples in the hold;
The sails were made of silk,
And the masts were made of gold.

The four-and-twenty sailors
That stood between the decks,
Were four-and-twenty white mice
With chains about their necks.

The captain was a duck,
With a packet on his back;
And when the ship began to move,
The captain said, "Quack! Quack!"

A WALNUT

As soft as silk, as white as milk,
As bitter as gall, a strong wall,
And a green coat covers me all.

THE MAN IN THE MOON

The Man in the Moon came tumbling
down,
And asked the way to Norwich;
He went by the south, and burnt his
mouth
With eating cold pease porridge.

ONE, HE LOVES

One, he loves; two, he loves:
Three, he loves, they say;
Four, he loves with all his heart;
Five, he casts away.
Six, he loves; seven, she loves;
Eight, they both love.
Nine, he comes; ten, he tarries;
Eleven, he courts; twelve, he mar-
ries.

BAT, BAT

Bat, bat,
Come under my hat,
And I'll give you a slice of bacon;
And when I bake
I'll give you a cake
If I am not mistaken.

HARK! HARK! THE DOGS DO BARK!

MY LOVE

Saw ye aught of my love a-coming
from the market?
A peck of meal upon her back,
A babby in her basket;
Saw ye aught of my love a-coming
from the market?

THE MAN OF BOMBAY

There was a fat man of Bombay,
Who was smoking one sunshiny day;
When a bird called a snipe
Flew away with his pipe,
Which vexed the fat man of Bombay

HARK! HARK!

Hark, hark! the dogs do bark!
Beggars are coming to town:
Some in jags, and some in rags,
And some in velvet gown.

THE HART

The hart he loves the high wood,
The hare she loves the hill;
The Knight he loves his bright
sword,
The Lady—loves her will.

MY MAID MARY

My maid Mary she minds the dairy,
  While I go a-hoeing and mowing
    each morn;
Gaily run the reel and the little
    spinning wheel.
  While I am singing and mowing
    my corn.

A DIFFICULT RHYME

What is the rhyme for porringer?
The king he had a daughter fair,
And gave the Prince of Orange her.

POOR OLD ROBINSON CRUSOE!

Poor old Robinson Crusoe!
Poor old Robinson Crusoe!
  They made him a coat
  Of an old Nanny goat.
I wonder why they should do so!
  With a ring-a-ting-tang,
  And a ring-a-ting-tang,
Poor old Robinson Crusoe!

A SIEVE

A riddle, a riddle, as I suppose,
A hundred eyes and never a nose!

PRETTY JOHN WATTS

Pretty John Watts,
We are troubled with rats.
Will you drive them out of the
  house?
We have mice, too, in plenty,
That feast in the pantry,
But let them stay
And nibble away,
What harm in a little brown mouse?

GOOD ADVICE

Come when you're called,
  Do what you're bid,
Shut the door after you,
  And never be chid.

I LOVE SIXPENCE

I love sixpence, a jolly, jolly
  sixpence,
  I love sixpence as my life;
I spent a penny of it, I spent a
  penny of it,
  I took a penny home to my
  wife.

Oh, my little fourpence, a jolly,
  jolly fourpence,
  I love fourpence as my life;
I spent twopence of it, I spent twopence of it,
  And I took twopence home to
  my wife.

BYE, BABY BUNTING

Bye, baby bunting,
Father's gone a-hunting,
Mother's gone a-milking,
Sister's gone a-silking,
And brother's gone to buy a skin
To wrap the baby bunting in.

TOM, TOM, THE PIPER'S SON

Tom, Tom, the piper's son,
Stole a pig, and away he run,
  The pig was eat,
  And Tom was beat,
And Tom ran crying down the
  street.

COMICAL FOLK

In a cottage in Fife
Lived a man and his wife
Who, believe me, were comical folk;
   For, to people's surprise,
   They both saw with their eyes,
And their tongues moved whenever
   they spoke!

When they were asleep,
I'm told, that to keep
Their eyes open they could not
   contrive;
   They both walked on their feet,
   And 'twas thought what they
   eat
Helped, with drinking, to keep them
   alive!

COCK-CROW

Cocks crow in the morn
      To tell us to rise,
And he who lies late
      Will never be wise;
For early to bed
      And early to rise,
Is the way to be healthy
      And wealthy and wise.

TOMMY SNOOKS

As Tommy Snooks and Bessy
   Brooks
   Were walking out one Sunday,
Says Tommy Snooks to Bessy
   Brooks,
   "Wilt marry me on Monday?"

COCK-CROW

THE THREE SONS

There was an old woman had three
    sons,
Jerry and James and John,
Jerry was hanged, James was
    drowned,
John was lost and never was found;
And there was an end of her three
    sons,
Jerry and James and John!

THE BLACKSMITH

"Robert Barnes, my fellow fine,
Can you shoe this horse of mine?"
"Yes, good sir, that I can,
As well as any other man;
There's a nail, and there's a prod,
Now, good sir, your horse is shod."

TWO GRAY KITS

The two gray kits,
And the gray kits' mother,
  All went over
The bridge together.

The bridge broke down,
  They all fell in;
"May the rats go with you,"
  Says Tom Bolin.

ONE, TWO, BUCKLE
MY SHOE

One, two,
Buckle my shoe;
Three, four,
Knock at the door;
Five, six,
Pick up sticks;
Seven, eight,
Lay them straight;
Nine, ten,
A good, fat hen;
Eleven, twelve,
Dig and delve;
Thirteen, fourteen,
Maids a-courting;
Fifteen, sixteen,
Maids in the kitchen;
Seventeen, eighteen,
Maids a-waiting;
Nineteen, twenty,
My plate's empty.

COCK-A-DOODLE-DO!

Cock-a-doodle-do!
My dame has lost her shoe,
My master's lost his fiddle-stick
And knows not what to do.

Cock-a-doodle-do!
What is my dame to do?
Till master finds his fiddle-stick,
She'll dance without her shoe.

PAIRS OR PEARS

Twelve pairs hanging high,
Twelve knights riding by,
Each knight took a pear,
And yet left a dozen there.

BELLEISLE

At the siege of Belleisle
I was there all the while,
All the while, all the while,
At the siege of Belleisle.

81

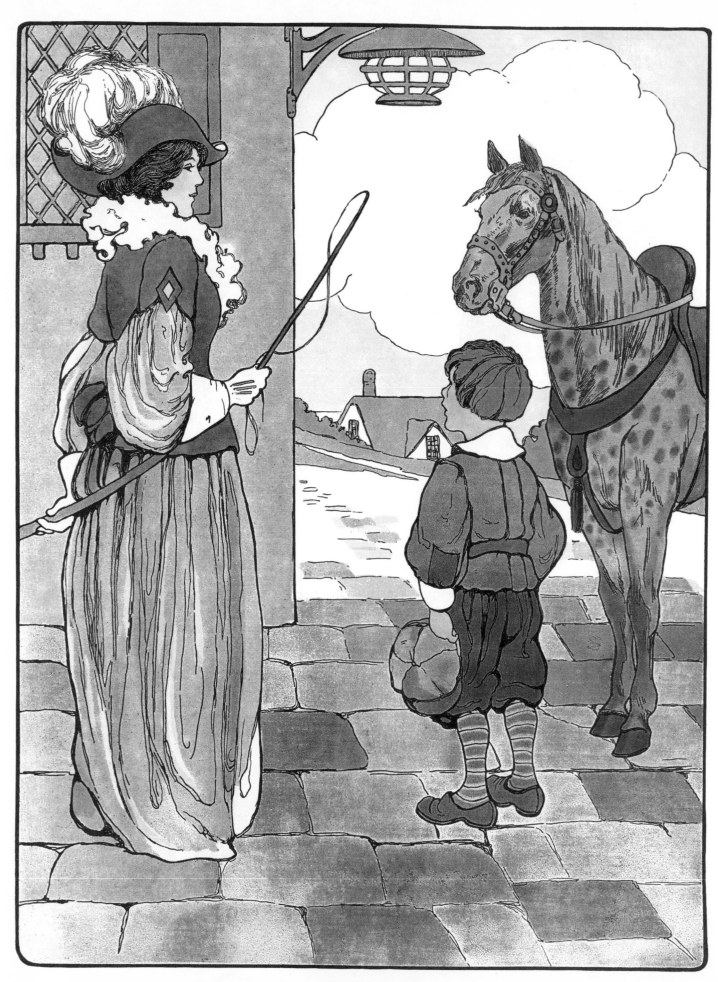

DAPPLE-GRAY

OLD KING COLE

Old King Cole
Was a merry old soul,
And a merry old soul was he;
He called for his pipe,
And he called for his bowl,
And he called for his fiddlers three!
And every fiddler, he had a fine
fiddle,
And a very fine fiddle had he.
"Twee tweedle dee, tweedle dee,"
went the fiddlers.
Oh, there's none so rare
As can compare
With King Cole and his fiddlers
three.

SEE, SEE

See, see! What shall I see?
A horse's head where his tail
should be.

DAPPLE-GRAY

I had a little pony,
His name was Dapple-Gray,
I lent him to a lady,
To ride a mile away.
She whipped him, she slashed him,
She rode him through the mire;
I would not lend my pony now
For all the lady's hire.

A WELL

As round as an apple, as deep as a
cup,
And all the king's horses can't fill
it up.

COFFEE AND TEA

Molly, my sister and I fell out,
And what do you think it was all
about?
She loved coffee and I loved tea,
And that was the reason we couldn't
agree.

PUSSY-CAT MEW

Pussy-cat Mew jumped over a coal,
And in her best petticoat burnt a
great hole.
Poor Pussy's weeping, she'll have
no more milk
Until her best petticoat's mended
with silk.

A COCK AND BULL STORY

The cock's on the housetop blowing
his horn;
The bull's in the barn a-threshing
of corn;
The maids in the meadows are
making of hay;
The ducks in the river are swim-
ming away.

FOR BABY

You shall have an apple,
YOU shall have a plum,
You shall have a rattle,
When papa comes home.

THE LITTLE GIRL WITH A CURL

There was a little girl who had a little
curl
Right in the middle of her forehead;
When she was good, she was very,
very good,
And when she was bad she was
horrid.

DREAMS

Friday night's dream, on Saturday
told,
Is sure to come true, be it never so
old.

OVER THE WATER

Over the water, and over the sea,
And over the water to Charley,
I'll have none of your nasty beef,
Nor I'll have none of your barley;
But I'll have some of your very best
    flour
To make a white cake for my
    Charley.

CANDLE-SAVING

To make your candles last for aye,
You wives and maids give ear-O!
To put them out's the only way,
Says honest John Boldero.

MYSELF

As I walked by myself,
And talked to myself,
    Myself said unto me:
"Look to thyself,
Take care of thyself,
    For nobody cares for thee."

I answered myself,
And said to myself
    In the selfsame repartee:
"Look to thyself,
Or not look to thyself,
    The selfsame thing will be."

LADYBIRD

FEARS AND TEARS

Tommy's tears and Mary's fears
Will make them old before their
years.

THE KILKENNY CATS

There were once two cats of
Kilkenny.
Each thought there was one cat too
many;
So they fought and they fit,
And they scratched and they bit,
Till, excepting their nails,
And the tips of their tails,
Instead of two cats, there weren't
any.

OLD GRIMES

Old Grimes is dead, that good old
man,
We ne'er shall see him more;
He used to wear a long brown coat
All buttoned down before.

A WEEK OF BIRTHDAYS

Monday's child is fair of face,
Tuesday's child is full of grace,
Wednesday's child is full of woe,
Thursday's child has far to go,
Friday's child is loving and giving,
Saturday's child works hard for its
living,
But the child that's born on the
Sabbath day
Is bonny and blithe, and good and
gay.

A CHIMNEY

Black within and red without;
Four corners round about.

LADYBIRD

Ladybird, ladybird, fly away home!
Your house is on fire, your children
all gone,
All but one, and her name is Ann,
And she crept under the pudding
pan.

THE MAN WHO HAD NAUGHT

There was a man and he had naught,
    And robbers came to rob him;
He crept up to the chimney pot,
    And then they thought they
        had him.

But he got down on t'other side,
    And then they could not find
        him;
He ran fourteen miles in fifteen days,
    And never looked behind him.

THE TAILORS AND THE SNAIL

Four and Twenty tailors
    Went to kill a snail;
The best man among them
    Durst not touch her tail;
She put out her horns
    Like a little Kyloe cow.
Run, tailors, run, or
    She'll kill you all e'en now.

AROUND THE GREEN GRAVEL

Around the green gravel the grass
    grows green,
And all the pretty maids are plain
    to be seen;
Wash them with milk, and clothe
    them with silk,
And write their names with a pen
    and ink.

INTERY, MINTERY

Intery, mintery, cutery corn,
Apple seed and apple thorn;
Wire, brier, limber-lock,
Five geese in a flock,
Sit and sing by a spring,
O-u-t, and in again.

CAESAR'S SONG

Bow-wow-wow!
Whose dog art thou?
Little Tom Tinker's dog,
Bow-wow-wow!

AS I WAS GOING ALONG

As I was going along, along,
A-singing a comical song, song, song,
The lane that I went was so long,
    long, long,
And the song that I sang was so
    long, long, long,
And so I went singing along.

HECTOR PROTECTOR

Hector Protector was dressed all in
    green;
Hector Protector was sent to the
    Queen.
The Queen did not like him,
No more did the King;
So Hector Protector was sent back
    again.

BILLY, BILLY

"Billy, Billy, come and play,
While the sun shines bright as day."

"Yes, my Polly, so I will,
For I love to please you still."

"Billy, Billy, have you seen
Sam and Betsy on the green?"

"Yes, my Poll, I saw them pass,
Skipping o'er the new-mown grass."

"Billy, Billy, come along,
And I will sing a pretty song."

ROCK-A-BYE, BABY

Rock-a-bye, baby, thy cradle is green;
Father's a nobleman, mother's a
    queen;
And Betty's a lady, and wears a
    gold ring;
And Johnny's a drummer, and
    drums for the king.

THE MAN IN THE WILDERNESS

The man in the wilderness
    Asked me
How many strawberries
    Grew in the sea.
I answered him
    As I thought good,
As many as red herrings
    Grew in the wood.

MARY, MARY, QUITE CONTRARY

Mary, Mary, quite contrary,
   How does your garden grow?
Silver bells and cockle-shells,
   And pretty maids all of a row.

BESSY BELL AND MARY GRAY

Bessy Bell and Mary Gray,
   They were two bonny lasses;
They built their house upon the lea,
   And covered it with rushes.

Bessy kept the garden gate,
   And Mary kept the pantry;
Bessy always had to wait,
   While Mary lived in plenty.

LITTLE JACK HORNER

Little Jack Horner
Sat in the corner,
   Eating of Christmas pie:
He put in his thumb,
And pulled out a plum,
   And said, "What a good boy
     am I!"

THE BIRD SCARER

Away, birds, away!
Take a little and leave a little,
And do not come again;
For if you do,
I will shoot you through,
And there will be an end of you.

MARY, MARY, QUITE CONTRARY

NEEDLES AND PINS

Needles and pins, needles and pins,
When a man marries his trouble
    begins.

PUSSY-CAT AND THE DUMPLINGS

Pussy-cat ate the dumplings, the
        dumplings,
    Pussy-cat ate the dumplings.
Mamma stood by, and cried, "Oh,
    fie!
    Why did you eat the dump-
lings?"

DANCE, THUMBKIN DANCE

Dance, Thumbkin, dance;
        (keep the thumb in motion
Dance, ye merrymen, everyone.
        (all the fingers in motion
For Thumbkin, he can dance alone,
        (the thumb alone moving
Thumbkin, he can dance alone.
        (the thumb alone moving
Dance, Foreman, dance,
        (the first finger moving
Dance, ye merrymen, everyone.
        (all moving
But Foreman, he can dance alone,
        (the first finger moving
Foreman, he can dance alone.
        (the first finger moving
Dance, Longman, dance,
        (the second finger moving
Dance, ye merrymen, everyone.
        (all moving
For Longman, he can dance alone,
        (the second finger moving
Longman, he can dance alone.
        (the second finger moving
Dance, Ringman, dance,
        (the third finger moving
Dance, ye merrymen, dance.
        (all moving
But Ringman cannot dance alone,
        (the third finger moving
Ringman, he cannot dance alone.
        (the third finger moving
Dance, Littleman, dance,
        (the fourth finger moving
Dance, ye merrymen, dance.
        (all moving
But Littleman, he can dance alone,
        (the fourth finger moving
Littleman, he can dance alone.
        (the fourth finger moving

THE LITTLE BIRD

Once I saw a little bird
    Come hop, hop, hop;
So I cried, "Little bird,
    Will you stop, stop, stop?"

And was going to the window
    To say, "How do you do?"
But he shook his little tail,
    And far away he flew.

BIRDS OF A FEATHER

Birds of a feather flock together,
    And so will pigs and swine;
Rats and mice will have their choice,
    And so will I have mine.

MARY'S CANARY

Mary had a pretty bird,
    Feathers bright and yellow,
Slender legs—upon my word
    He was a pretty fellow!

The sweetest note he always sung,
    Which much delighted Mary.
She often, where the cage was hung,
    Sat hearing her canary.

THE DUSTY MILLER

Margaret wrote a letter,
Sealed it with her finger,
Threw it in the dam
For the dusty miller.
Dusty was his coat,
Dusty was the siller,
Dusty was the kiss
I'd from the dusty miller.
If I had my pockets
Full of gold and siller,
I would give it all
To my dusty miller.

A STAR

Higher than a house, higher
    than a tree.
Oh! whatever can that be?

THE GREEDY MAN

The greedy man is he who sits
    And bites bits out of plates,
Or else takes up an almanac
    And gobbles all the dates.

THE TEN O'CLOCK
SCHOLAR

A diller, a dollar, a ten o'clock scholar!
    What makes you come so soon?
You used to come at ten o'clock,
    But now you come at noon.

THE TEN O'CLOCK SCHOLAR

COCK-A-DOODLE-DO

Oh, my pretty cock, oh, my handsome cock,
    I pray you, do not crow before day,
And your comb shall be made of the very
        beaten gold,
    And your wings of the silver so gray.

AN ICICLE

Lives in winter,
Dies in summer,
And grows with its roots upward!

A SHIP'S NAIL

Over the water,
And under the water,
And always with its head down.

THE OLD WOMAN OF LEEDS

There was an old woman of Leeds,
Who spent all her time in good
deeds;
She worked for the poor
Till her fingers were sore,
This pious old woman of Leeds!

THE BOY IN THE BARN

A little boy went into a barn,
And lay down on some hay.
An owl came out, and flew about,
And the little boy ran away.

SUNSHINE

Hick-a-more, Hack-a-more,
On the King's kitchen door,
All the King's horses,
And all the King's men,
Couldn't drive Hick-a-more,
Hack-a-more,
Off the King's kitchen door.

WILLY, WILLY

Willy, Willy Wilkin
Kissed the maids a-milking,
Fa, la, la!
And with his merry daffing
He set them all a-laughing,
Ha, ha, ha!

THE QUARREL

My little old man and I fell out;
I 'll tell you what 'twas all about,—
I had money and he had none,
And that's the way the noise begun.

THE PUMPKIN-EATER

Peter, Peter, pumpkin-eater,
Had a wife and couldn't keep her;
He put her in a pumpkin shell,
And there he kept her very well.

TONGS

Long legs, crooked thighs,
Little head, and no eyes.

JACK JINGLE

Little Jack Jingle,
He used to live single;
But when he got tired of this
kind of life,
He left off being single and
lived with his wife.
Now what do you think of
little Jack Jingle?
Before he was married he used
to live single.

PETER, PETER, PUMPKIN-EATER

THAT'S ALL

There was an old woman sat spinning,
And that's the first beginning;

She had a calf,
And that's half;

She took it by the tail,
And threw it over the wall,
And that's all!

SHOEING

Shoe the colt,
Shoe the colt,
Shoe the wild mare;
Here a nail,
There a nail,
Yet she goes bare.

BETTY BLUE

Little Betty Blue
Lost her holiday shoe;
What shall little Betty do?
Give her another
To match the other
And then she'll walk upon two.

BEDTIME

The Man in the Moon looked
    out of the moon,
    Looked out of the moon
      and said,
"'Tis time for all children
      on the earth
    To think about getting to bed!"

DANCE, LITTLE BABY

Dance, little Baby, dance up high!
Never mind, Baby, Mother is by.
Crow and caper, caper and crow,
There, little Baby, there you go!
Up to the ceiling, down to the
    ground,
Backwards and forwards, round
    and round;
Dance, little Baby and Mother
    will sing,
With the merry coral, ding, ding,
    ding!

MY LITTLE MAID

High diddle doubt, my candle's
    out
    My little maid is not at home;
Saddle my hog and bridle my
    dog,
    And fetch my little maid
    home.

FOR WANT OF A NAIL

For want of a nail, the shoe was lost;
For want of the shoe, the horse was
    lost;
For want of the horse, the rider was
    lost;
For want of the rider, the battle was
    lost;
For want of the battle, the kingdom
    was lost,
And all for the want of a horseshoe
    nail.

THE CROOKED SIXPENCE

There was a crooked man, and he
went a crooked mile,
He found a crooked sixpence be-
side a crooked stile;
He bought a crooked cat, which
caught a crooked mouse,
And they all lived together in a
little crooked house.

THIS IS THE WAY

This is the way the ladies ride,
    Tri, tre, tre, tree,
    Tri, tre, tre, tree!
This is the way the ladies ride,
    Tri, tre, tre, tre, tri-tre-tre-tree!

This is the way the gentlemen ride,
    Gallop-a-trot,
    Gallop-a-trot!
This is the way the gentlemen ride,
    Gallop-a-gallop-a-trot!

This is the way the farmers ride,
    Hobbledy-hoy,
    Hobbledy-hoy!
This is the way the farmers ride,
    Hobbledy-hobbledy-hoy!

PEASE PORRIDGE

Pease porridge hot,
    Pease porridge cold,
Pease porridge in the pot,
    Nine days old.
Some like it hot,
    Some like it cold,
Some like it in the pot,
    Nine days old.

RING A RING O' ROSES

Ring a ring o' roses,
A pocketful of posies.
Tisha! Tisha!
We all fall down.

PEASE PORRIDGE HOT

DUCKS AND DRAKES

A duck and a drake,
And a halfpenny cake,
With a penny to pay the old baker.

A hop and a scotch
Is another notch,
Slitherum, slatherum, take her.

THE DONKEY

Donkey, donkey, old and gray,
Ope your mouth and gently bray;
Lift your ears and blow your horn,
To wake the world this sleepy
    morn.

IF

If all the world were apple pie,
And all the sea were ink,
And all the trees were bread and
    cheese,
What should we have for drink?

THE BELLS

"You owe me five shillings,"
Say the bells of St. Helen's.

"When will you pay me?"
Say the bells of Old Bailey.

"When I grow rich,"
Say the bells of Shoreditch.

"When will that be?"
Say the bells of Stepney.

"I do not know,"
Says the great Bell of Bow.

"Two sticks in an apple,"
Ring the bells of Whitechapel.

"Halfpence and farthings,"
Say the bells of St. Martin's.

"Kettles and pans,"
Say the bells of St. Ann's.

"Brickbats and tiles,"
Say the bells of St. Giles.

"Old shoes and slippers,"
Say the bells of St. Peter's.

"Pokers and tongs,"
Say the bells of St. John's.

LITTLE GIRL AND QUEEN

"Little girl, little girl, where have
    you been?"
"Gathering roses to give to the
    Queen."
"Little girl, little girl, what gave
    she you?"
"She gave me a diamond as big as
    my shoe."

THE KING OF FRANCE

The King of France went up the
    hill,
    With twenty thousand men;
The King of France came down the
    hill,
    And ne'er went up again.

THE TARTS

PETER PIPER

Peter Piper picked a peck of
pickled peppers;
A peck of pickled peppers Peter
Piper picked.
If Peter Piper picked a peck of
pickled peppers,
Where's the peck of pickled peppers
Peter Piper picked?

ONE TO TEN

1, 2, 3, 4, 5!
I caught a hare alive;
6, 7, 8, 9, 10!
I let her go again.

AN EQUAL

Read my riddle, I pray.
What God never sees,
What the king seldom sees,
What we see every day.

THE TARTS

The Queen of Hearts,
She made some tarts,
All on a summer's day;
The Knave of Hearts,
He stole the tarts,
And took them clean away.

The King of Hearts
Called for the tarts,
And beat the Knave full sore;
The Knave of Hearts
Brought back the tarts,
And vowed he'd steal no more.

WHAT ARE LITTLE BOYS MADE OF?

What are little boys made of, made of?
What are little boys made of?
"Snaps and snails, and puppy-dogs' tails;
And that's what little boys are made of."

What are little girls made of, made of?
What are little girls made of?
"Sugar and spice, and all that's nice;
And that's what little girls are made of."

COME, LET'S TO BED

"To bed! To bed!"
　　Says Sleepy-head;
"Tarry awhile," says Slow;
"Put on the pan,"
　　Says Greedy Nan;
　　"We'll sup before we go."

LITTLE MAID

"Little maid, pretty maid, whither goest thou?"
"Down in the forest to milk my cow."
'Shall I go with thee?"　"No, not now;
When I send for thee, then come thou."

So I went into Darlington, that pretty little town,
And there I bought a petticoat, a cloak, and a gown.

I went into the woods and built me a kirk,
And all the birds of the air, they helped me to work.

The hawk with his long claws pulled down the stone,
The dove with her rough bill brought me them home.

The parrot was the clergyman, the peacock was the clerk,
The bullfinch played the organ, — we made merry work.

BANDY LEGS

As I was going to sell my eggs
I met a man with bandy legs,
Bandy legs and crooked toes;
I tripped up his heels, and he fell on his nose.

THE GIRL AND THE BIRDS

When I was a little girl, about seven years old,
I had n't got a petticoat, to cover me from the cold.

A PIG

As I went to Bonner,
I met a pig
Without a wig
Upon my word and honor.

JENNY WREN

As little Jenny Wren
    Was sitting by her shed.
She waggled with her tail,
    And nodded with her head.
She waggled with her tail,
    And nodded with her head,
As little Jenny Wren
    Was sitting by the shed.

LITTLE TOM TUCKER

Little Tom Tucker
    Sings for his supper.
What shall he eat?
    White bread and butter.
How will he cut it
    Without e'er a knife?
How will he be married
    Without e'er a wife?

LITTLE TOM TUCKER

WHERE ARE YOU GOING, MY PRETTY MAID

"Where are you going, my pretty maid?"

"I'm going a-milking, sir," she said.

"May I go with you, my pretty maid?"

"You're kindly welcome, sir," she said.

"What is your father, my pretty maid?"

"My father's a farmer, sir," she said.

"What is your fortune, my pretty maid?"

"My face is my fortune, sir," she said.

"Then I can't marry you, my pretty maid."

"Nobody asked you, sir," she said.

THE OLD WOMAN OF GLOUCESTER

There was an old woman of Gloucester,

Whose parrot two guineas it cost her,

But its tongue never ceasing,

Was vastly displeasing

To the talkative woman of Gloucester.

MULTIPLICATION IS VEXATION

Multiplication is vexation,
    Division is as bad;
The Rule of Three doth puzzle me,
    And Practice drives me mad.

LITTLE KING BOGGEN

Little King Boggen, he built a fine
    hall,
Pie-crust and pastry-crust, that was
    the wall;
The windows were made of black
    puddings and white,
And slated with pan-cakes,—you
    ne'er saw the like!

WHISTLE

"Whistle, daughter, whistle;
    Whistle, daughter dear."
"I cannot whistle, mammy,
    I cannot whistle clear."
"Whistle, daughter, whistle;
    Whistle for a pound."
"I cannot whistle, mammy,
    I cannot make a sound."

BELL HORSES

Bell horses, bell horses, what
    time of day?
One o'clock, two o'clock, three
    and away.

TAFFY

Taffy was a Welshman, Taffy was
    a thief,
Taffy came to my house and stole a
    piece of beef;
I went to Taffy's house, Taffy was
    not home;
Taffy came to my house and stole a
    marrow-bone.

I went to Taffy's house, Taffy was
    not in;
Taffy came to my house and stole a
    silver pin;
I went to Taffy's house, Taffy was
    in bed,
I took up the marrow-bone and
    flung it at his head.

YOUNG ROGER AND DOLLY

Young Roger came tapping at
　　Dolly's window,
　　Thumpaty, thumpaty, thump!

He asked for admittance; she
　　answered him "No!"
　　Frumpaty, frumpaty, frump!

"No, no, Roger, no! as you came
　　you may go!"
　　Stumpaty, stumpaty, stump!

THE ROBIN

The north wind doth blow,
And we shall have snow,
And what will poor robin do then,
　　　　　　Poor thing?
He'll sit in a barn,
And keep himself warm,
And hide his head under his wing,
　　　　　　Poor thing!

THE OLD WOMAN OF
HARROW

There was an old woman of
　　Harrow,
Who visited in a wheelbarrow;
　　And her servant before,
　　Knocked loud at each door,
To announce the old woman of
　　Harrow.

114

YOUNG ROGER AND DOLLY

THE COACHMAN

Up at Piccadilly, oh!
   The coachman takes his stand,
And when he meets a pretty girl
   He takes her by the hand;
Whip away forever, oh!
   Drive away so clever, oh!
All the way to Bristol, oh!
   He drives her four-in-hand.

THERE WAS AN OLD WOMAN

There was an old woman who lived
   in a shoe.
She had so many children she
   didn't know what to do.
She gave them some broth without
   any bread.
She whipped them all soundly and
   put them to bed.

THE PIPER AND HIS COW

There was a piper had a cow,
   And he had naught to give her;
He pulled out his pipes and played
    her a tune,
   And bade the cow consider.

The cow considered very well,
   And gave the piper a penny,
And bade him play the other tune,
   "Corn rigs are bonny."

THE MAN OF DERBY

A little old man of Derby,
How do you think he served me?
He took away my bread and cheese,
And that is how he served me.

A THORN

I went to the wood and got it;
I sat me down to look for it
And brought it home because I
    couldn't find it.

THE OLD WOMAN OF SURREY

There was an old woman in Surrey,
Who was morn, noon, and night
    in a hurry;
    Called her husband a fool,
    Drove the children to school,
The worrying old woman of Surrey.

THE LITTLE MOUSE

I have seen you, little mouse,

Running all about the house,

Through the hole your little eye

In the wainscot peeping sly,

Hoping soon some crumbs to steal,

To make quite a hearty meal.

Look before you venture out,

See if pussy is about.

If she's gone, you'll quickly run

To the larder for some fun;

Round about the dishes creep,

Taking into each a peep,

To choose the daintiest that's there,

Spoiling things you do not care.

117

BOY AND GIRL

There was a little boy and a
    little girl
Lived in an alley;
Says the little boy to the little
    girl,
    "Shall I, oh, shall I?"
Says the little girl to the little
    boy,
    "What shall we do?"
Says the little boy to the little
    girl,
    "I will kiss you."

WHEN

When I was
    a bachelor
I lived by
    myself;
And all the
    bread and
    cheese I got
I laid up on the
    shelf.

The rats and the mice
    They made such a strife,
I was forced to go to London
    To buy me a wife.

The streets were so bad,
    And the lanes were so narrow,
I was forced to bring my wife home
    In a wheelbarrow.

The wheelbarrow broke,
    And my wife had a fall;
Down came wheelbarrow,
    Little wife and all.

WHEN I WAS A BACHELOR

SING, SING

Sing, sing, what shall I
    sing?
Cat's run away with the
    pudding-string!
Do, do, what shall I
    do?
The cat has bitten it
    quite in two.

LONDON BRIDGE

London Bridge is broken down,
Dance over my Lady Lee;
London Bridge is broken down,
With a gay lady.

How shall we build it up again?
Dance over my Lady Lee;
How shall we build it up again?
With a gay lady.

Build it up with silver and gold,
Dance over my Lady Lee;
Build it up with silver and gold,
With a gay lady.

Silver and gold will be stole away,
Dance over my Lady Lee;
Silver and gold will be stole away,
With a gay lady.

Build it up with iron and steel,
Dance over my Lady Lee;
Build it up with iron and steel,
With a gay lady.

Iron and steel will bend and bow,
Dance over my Lady Lee;
Iron and steel will bend and bow,
With a gay lady.

Build it up with wood and clay,
Dance over my Lady Lee;
Build it up with wood and clay,
With a gay lady.

Wood and clay will wash away,
Dance over my Lady Lee;
Wood and clay will wash away,
With a gay lady.

Build it up with stone so strong,
Dance over my Lady Lee;
Huzza! 'twill last for ages long,
With a gay lady.

MARCH WINDS

March winds and April showers
Bring forth May flowers.

THE LOST SHOE

Doodle doodle doo,
The Princess lost her shoe:
   Her Highness hopped,—
   The fiddler stopped,
Not knowing what to do.

HOT CODLINS

There was a little woman, as I've
   been told,
Who was not very young, nor yet
   very old;
Now this little woman her living got
By selling codlins, hot, hot, hot!

THE BALLOON

"What is the news of the day,
Good neighbor, I pray?"
"They say the balloon
Is gone up to the moon!"

A CHERRY

As I went through the garden gap,
Who should I meet but Dick Red-
   cap!
A stick in his hand, a stone in his
   throat,—
If you'll tell me this riddle, I'll
   give you a groat.

SWAN

Swan, swan, over the sea;
Swim, swan, swim!
Swan, swan, back again;
Well swum, swan!

THREE STRAWS

Three straws on a staff
Would make a baby cry and laugh.

THE MAN OF TOBAGO

There was an old man of Tobago
Who lived on rice, gruel, and sago,
Till much to his bliss,
His physician said this:
"To a leg, sir, of mutton, you may
go."

DING, DONG, BELL

Ding, dong, bell,
Pussy's in the well!
Who put her in?
Little Tommy Lin.

Who pulled her out?
Little Johnny Stout.
What a naughty boy was that,
To try to drown poor pussy-cat.
Who never did him any harm,
But killed the mice in his father's
barn!

A SUNSHINY SHOWER

A sunshiny shower
Won't last half an hour.

The mischievous raven flew laugh-
ing away,
Bumpety, bumpety, bump!
And vowed he would serve them
the same the next day,
Lumpety, lumpety lump!

CHRISTMAS

Christmas is coming, the geese are
getting fat,
Please to put a penny in an old
man's hat;
If you haven't got a penny a
ha'penny will do,
If you haven't got a ha'penny, God
bless you.

THE FARMER AND THE RAVEN

A farmer went trotting upon his
gray mare,
Bumpety, bumpety, bump!
With his daughter behind him so
rosy and fair,
Lumpety, lumpety, lump!

A raven cried croak! and they all
tumbled down,
Bumpety, bumpety, bump!
The mare broke her knees, and the
farmer his crown,
Lumpety, lumpety, lump!

WILLY BOY

"Willy boy, Willy boy, where are
   you going?
I will go with you, if that I
   may."
"I'm going to the meadow to
   see them a-mowing,
I'm going to help them to make
   the hay."

POLLY AND SUKEY

Polly, put the kettle on,
Polly, put the kettle on,
Polly, put the kettle on,
      And let's drink tea.

Sukey, take it off again,
Sukey, take it off again,
Sukey, take it off again,
      They're all gone away.

THE DEATH AND BURIAL
OF POOR COCK ROBIN

Who killed Cock Robin?
"I," said the sparrow,
"With my little bow and arrow,
I killed Cock Robin."

Who saw him die?
"I," said the fly,
"With my little eye,
I saw him die."

Who caught his blood?
"I," said the fish,
"With my little dish,
I caught his blood."

Who'll make his shroud?
"I," said the beetle,
"With my thread and needle.
I'll make his shroud."

Who'll carry the torch?
"I," said the linnet,
"I'll come in a minute,
I'll carry the torch."

Who'll be the clerk?
"I," said the lark,
"If it's not in the dark,
I'll be the clerk."

Who'll dig his grave?
"I," said the owl,
"With my spade and trowel
I'll dig his grave."

Who'll be the parson?
"I," said the rook,
"With my little book,
I'll be the parson."

Who'll be chief mourner?
"I," said the dove,
"I mourn for my love,
I'll be chief mourner."

Who'll sing a psalm?
"I," said the thrush,
"As I sit in a bush.
I'll sing a psalm."

Who'll carry the coffin?
"I," said the kite,
"If it's not in the night,
I'll carry the coffin."

Who'll toll the bell?
"I," said the bull,
"Because I can pull,
I'll toll the bell."

All the birds of the air
Fell sighing and sobbing,
When they heard the bell toll
For poor Cock Robin.

THE MOUSE AND THE CLOCK

Hickory, dickory, dock!
The mouse ran up the clock;
The clock struck one,
And down he run,
Hickory, dickory, dock!

THE BUNCH OF BLUE RIBBONS

THE BUNCH OF BLUE RIBBONS

Oh, dear, what can the matter be?
Oh, dear, what can the matter be?
Oh, dear, what can the matter be?
    Johnny's so long at the fair.

He promised he'd buy me a bunch
    of blue ribbons,
He promised he'd buy me a bunch
    of blue ribbons,
He promised he'd buy me a bunch
    of blue ribbons,
    To tie up my bonny brown
    hair.

HOT-CROSS BUNS

    Hot-cross Buns!
    Hot-cross Buns!
One a penny, two a penny,
    Hot-cross Buns!
    Hot-cross Buns!
    Hot-cross Buns!
If ye have no daughters,
Give them to your sons.

BOBBY SHAFTOE

Bobby Shaftoe's gone to sea,
With silver buckles on his knee:
He'll come back and marry me,
    Pretty Bobby Shaftoe!
Bobby Shaftoe's fat and fair,
Combing down his yellow hair;
He's my love for evermore,
    Pretty Bobby Shaftoe.

THE WOMAN OF EXETER

There dwelt an old woman at Exeter;
When visitors came it sore vexed her,
    So for fear they should eat,
    She locked up all her meat,
This stingy old woman of Exeter.

SNEEZING

If you sneeze on Monday, you
    sneeze for danger;
Sneeze on a Tuesday, kiss a
    stranger;
Sneeze on a Wednesday, sneeze for
    a letter;
Sneeze on a Thursday, something
    better.
Sneeze on a Friday, sneeze for
    sorrow;
Sneeze on a Saturday, joy to-
    morrow.

PUSSY-CAT BY THE FIRE

Pussy-cat sits by the fire;
    How can she be fair?
In walks the little dog;
    Says: "Pussy, are you there?
How do you do, Mistress Pussy?
    Mistress Pussy, how d'ye do?"
"I thank you kindly, little dog,
    I fare as well as you!"

WHEN THE SNOW IS ON THE GROUND

The little robin grieves
    When the snow is on the ground,
For the trees have no leaves,
    And no berries can be found.
The air is cold, the worms are hid;
    For robin here what can be
    done?
Let's strow around some crumbs of
    bread,
    And then he'll live till snow is
    gone.